Harper and the Big

T0364464

Written by Sarah Snashall

Illustrated by Alfredo Belli

Collins

Storm is a big dog. He prowls in the next garden and he frightens me.

I can not sleep when I can hear him bark and growl.

Mum and I go up the steep steps to avoid Storm's house.

Stop it, Storm!

4

A big brown dog bursts from the trees.
A little dog trails him.

CRASH!

The little dog snaps and snarls at the big dog. I screech with fright.

I hear the big dog start to howl and growl. It is Storm!

Storm groans and creeps next to Mum and me. The little dog frightens him!

I look at Storm. My fear starts
to vanish. Storm has had a fright,
just like me.

At night, I hear Storm growl and prowl.
Perhaps he has seen a slug or a snail!

Soon I will spoil him with a trip and a snack.

Harper and Storm

 After reading

Letters and Sounds: Phase 4

Word count: 170

Focus on adjacent consonants with long vowel phonemes, e.g. *speed*.

Common exception words: the, what, there, when, I, he, me, house, little, you, to, go, like

Curriculum links (National Curriculum, Year 1): Science: Animals, including humans

National Curriculum learning objectives: Reading/word reading: apply phonic knowledge and skills as the route to decode words; read accurately by blending sounds in unfamiliar words containing GPCs that have been taught; Reading/comprehension: understand both the books they can already read accurately and fluently and those they listen to by making inferences on the basis of what is being said and done

Developing fluency

- Take turns to read a page, ensuring your child pays attention to full stops and pauses before starting each new sentence.
- Encourage your child to read with expression, noting the exclamation marks as an instruction to emphasise the sentence or word, or read with a tone of surprise.

Phonic practice

- Practise reading words with more than one consonant at the beginning and/or end of the words:

  trails   crash   fright   screech   snarls   stand

- Challenge your child to read the following two syllable words. Can they identify the syllables in each?

  a/fraid   gar/den   fright/ens   growl/ing   groan/ing   per/haps

Extending vocabulary

- Ask your child to suggest a synonym or a phrase that explains the meaning of each word:
  - prowls (e.g. *creeps; moves slowly and secretly*)
  - afraid (e.g. *scared; be very nervous*)
  - groans (e.g. *moans; makes a deep noise*)